UPTOWN

Bryan Collier

H **Square Fish**

Imprints of Macmillan
175 Fifth Avenue
New York, New York 10010
mackids.com

Henry Holt® is a registered trademark of Henry Holt and Company, LLC. *Publishers since 1866.*
Square Fish and the Square Fish logo are trademarks of Macmillan and
are used by Henry Holt and Company under license from Macmillan.

Library of Congress Cataloging-in-Publication Data
Collier, Bryan.
Uptown / Bryan Collier.
p.   cm.
Summary: A tour of the sights of Harlem, including the Metro-North train, brownstones, shopping on
125th Street, a barbershop, summer basketball, the Harlem Boys Choir, and sunset over the Hudson River.
[1. Harlem (New York, N.Y.)—Fiction. 2. Afro-Americans—Fiction.] I. Title.
PZ7.C67734Up 2000   [E]—dc21   99-31774

ISBN 978-0-8050-5721-6 (Henry Holt hardcover)
9   10

ISBN 978-0-8050-7399-7 (Square Fish paperback)
15   17   19   20   18   16   14

Originally published in the United States by Henry Holt and Company
Book designed by Martha Rago
The artist used watercolor and collage to create the illustrations for this book.
First Square Fish Edition: November 2012
Square Fish logo designed by Filomena Tuosto

AR: 2.6 / LEXILE: AD420L

Dedicated to the loving memory of
my mother, Esther Collier.
To God be the Glory.

Uptown is a caterpillar.

Well, it's really the Metro-North train
as it eases over the Harlem River.

Uptown is chicken and waffles served around the clock.

At first it seems like a weird combination, but it works.

Uptown is a row of brownstones.

I like the way they come together
when you look at them down the block.
They look like they're made of chocolate.

Uptown
is
weekend shopping
on
125th Street.

The vibe is always jumping
as people bounce to their own
rhythms.

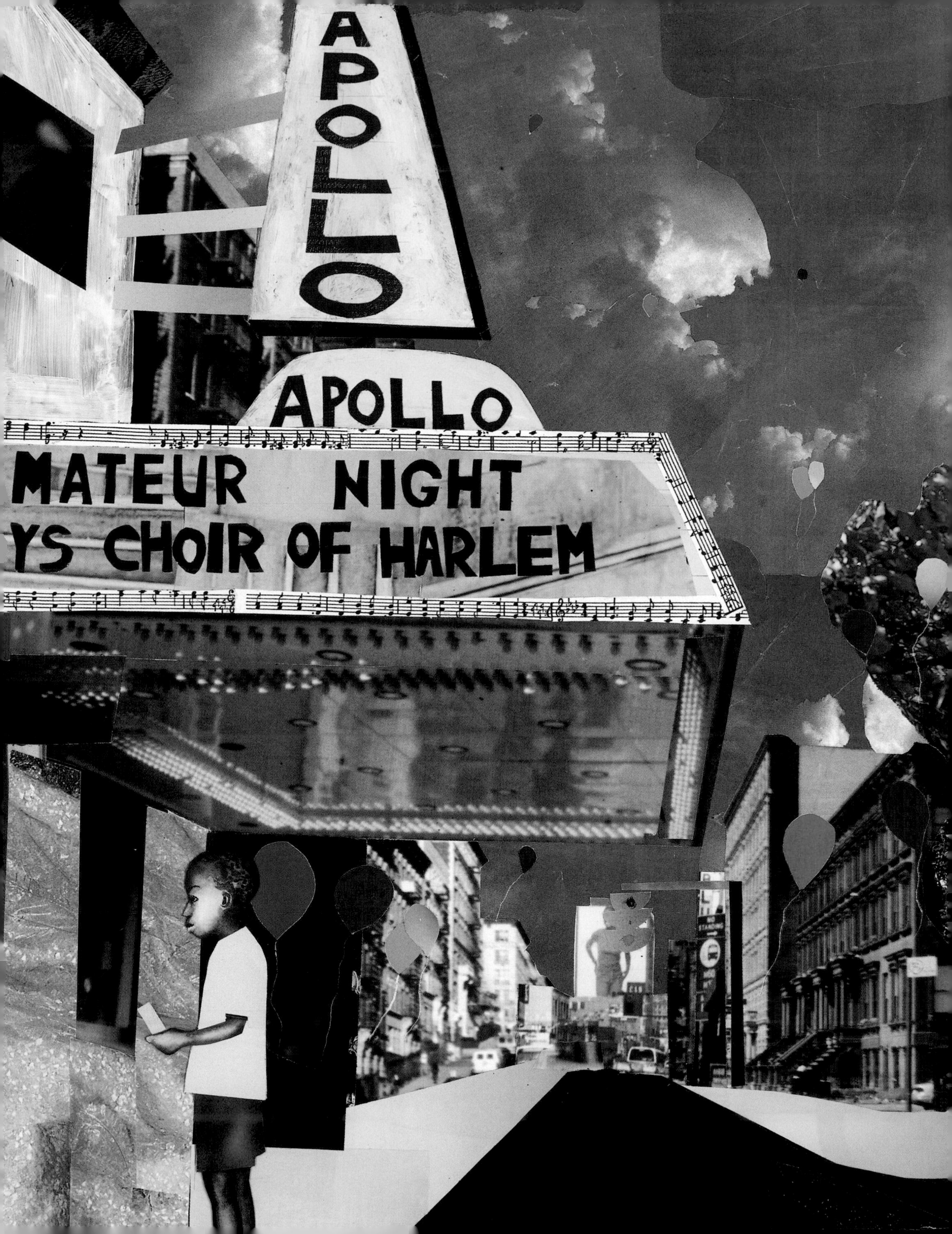
APOLLO
APOLLO
MATEUR NIGHT
YS CHOIR OF HARLEM

Uptown is a stage.

**The Apollo Theater
has showcased the greatest
entertainers in the world.**

I hope we can get good seats.

My grandfather says, "Jazz and Harlem are a perfect match—just like chicken and waffles."

Uptown is a barbershop.

It's a place where last night's ball game can be more important than what style haircut you want.

Uptown

is a

Van Der Zee

photograph.

I saw a picture from before my dad was even born—a picture of my grandparents' wedding day!

Uptown is summer basketball at the Ruckers.

at the Ruckers.

Anyone can rise up
and be a superstar for a day.

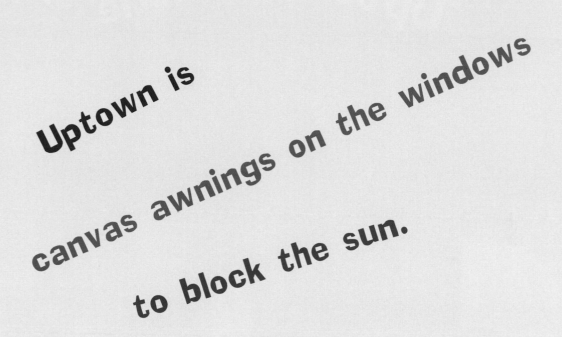

Uptown is
canvas awnings on the windows
to block the sun.

It's like the buildings are all dressed up.

They're on their way to church in matching yellow dresses.

Uptown
is the
orange sunset
over the
Hudson River.

That means it's time for the streetlights
to come on and for me to get home
and get changed.

Uptown is
a **song** sung
by the Boys Choir
of Harlem.

Each

note

floats through the air

and lands

like a butterfly.

Harlem world, my world.

Uptown is home.